Brockworth Library, Moorfield Road,
Brockworth, Gloucester. GL3 4EX
Tel: 01452 863681 Email:
office@brockworthlink.org.uk
www.brockworthlink.org.uk

**Brockworth
link**

**Items should be returned to any Gloucestershire County Library on or
before the date stamped below. This book remains the property of the
Brockworth Community Library and can be renewed in person or by
telephone by calling 01452 862 730**

04/24   Green/Brown

This edition first published in 2017 by Alligator Products Ltd
Cupcake is an imprint of Alligator Products Ltd,
2nd Floor, 314 Regents Park Road, London, N3 2JX
www.alligatorbooks.co.uk

Printed in China   0634

Olivia's Feathers

Written by Christine Swift
Illustrated by Claire Stimpson

cupcake

When Olivia Owl was born,
she was a beautiful little owl.

Olivia had huge, bright eyes and soft, grey fluffy feathers.

But Olivia
wanted to be
like her mummy.

Olivia loved her mummy's brown, silky feathers and her elegant wings.

In the night, Olivia's mummy would call her, "Twit, twoo".

Her mummy could swoop through the night sky, diving through the darkness and perching on the highest tree-tops.

Olivia felt safe when her mummy was near.

Best of all, Olivia loved to snuggle up with her mummy while she was sleeping.

"How can I be like you, mummy?"
asked Olivia.

"Oh Olivia, you are perfect just the way you are!" *said her mummy.*

When Olivia was sleeping, she dreamed
that she was just like her mummy.
In her dream she had brown feathers.

It felt amazing to fly through the darkness and
see her forest friends running below in the night.

Olivia had an idea. Every time her mummy lost one of her feathers, Olivia collected them.

The forest animals helped Olivia gather feathers.

Soon they had a huge pile.

*Everyone helped Olivia
with her transformation.*

The mice helped with Olivia's delicate wings.

Soon, Olivia was covered in brown feathers, just like in her dreams. All the animals marvelled at the 'new' Olivia!

"Look mummy, now I am just like you!" *giggled Olivia.*

Olivia showed off her new feathers.

Olivia's mummy laughed, **"You will always be my beautiful Olivia."**

Olivia looked at the brown feathers - she did feel a bit silly.

Olivia thought carefully, "I don't want these feathers any more, mummy."

Olivia's mummy helped her remove the feathers, and they watched them blow away. Soon Olivia could see her beautiful self!

"That was fun", *laughed Olivia,*
"but I am happy being ME!"

"and I love you just the way
you are" *said her mummy.*

Olivia called her friends,
"It's me, Olivia, I'm back!"
she giggled.

Her friends laughed, they loved Olivia because she was so much fun.

Olivia played with her little owl friends until bedtime.

Then Olivia's favourite thing of all - a bedtime snuggle from her mummy!